Newsman Ned Meets the New Family

by Steven Kroll • Pictures by Denise Brunkus

SCHOLASTIC INC.

New York Toronto London Auckland Sydney

ISBN 0-590-41367-8

Text copyright © 1988 by Steven Kroll.

Illustrations copyright © 1988 by Denise Brunkus.

Design by Claire Counihan.

All rights reserved. Published by Scholastic Inc.

12 11 10 9 8 7 6 5 4 3 2 1   8 9/8 0 1 2 3/9

Printed in the U.S.A.

First Scholastic printing, September 1988

It was early in the morning in Breezy Valley. Newsman
Ned stopped by Cathy's Cozy Corners Luncheonette for a
cup of coffee.

"Heard about the new family moving into the house on Grove Street?" Cathy asked.

"No," said Ned. "I haven't."

"They're different," said Cathy's daughter Ann. "Yesterday the movers brought in a trampoline, a bathtub with lion's feet, and a whole bunch of musical instruments."

"Maybe they're a show business family!" Ned said.

"That would be exciting," said Cathy, "but I hope they're not too busy to spend time with their kids. That's the best part of being a family."

"You bet," said Ned. "Thanks, Cathy. This sounds like a story for the *Breezy Valley Times*. Come on, Pete!"

Ned's floppy-eared dog Pete raced out the door with him. They jumped into Ned's old car. Right away they were stuck in traffic on Main Street.

Horns were honking. Drivers were yelling. Ned finally reached the crossing as the light changed for the third time.

Officer Ollie Burns was trying to calm tempers.

"You should have seen that van," he said. "It stalled at the light, and a big elephant's trunk came poking out the door."

"Was it a real elephant?" Ned asked.

"I think so," said Ollie, "but I only caught a glimpse of it. They pushed the trunk right back in."

"I bet that's the new family's moving van," said Ned. "Maybe they're in the circus!"

"Circus? My four kids are crazy about the circus. I just wish we could keep them in the same place for more than a minute."

"You and Marge do a very good job."

"Thanks. The kids all help each other, though."

The light changed. "'Bye, Ollie, gotta go," said Ned, and he and Pete drove off.

When they reached the house on Grove Street, the van was parked in the driveway. Pete dashed across the lawn. No one was around, but the front doors of the house were wide open.

Ned walked up the steps and went inside. The trampoline was in the front room. Ned imagined an acrobat mother and children doing flips in the air. In the bathroom at the top of the stairs was the tub with the lion's feet. Ned imagined a real lion taking a bath.

He walked into the next room. It was filled with spotlights. He imagined a ringmaster father practicing a speech under the lights.

Ned made some notes on his pad. "This is going to be some story!" he said. "Circus family moves to Breezy Valley!"

Then he heard Pete barking. On the lawn was a ball with a smiling clown face. Beside it was a set of rings, the kind someone might swing from.

Pete was jumping up and down. "Good boy, Pete, good boy," Ned said.

But where was everyone?

Ned drove down the road to Herb Jackson's garage. Maybe Herb would know the answer.

Herb waved hello. In his other hand he still held the gas pump. A tiny orange car had just driven away.

"There's a whole family in that car," said Herb.

Ned remembered the little car at the circus with all the clowns jumping out of it. "How many were there?" he asked. "What did they look like? Were they going to Grove Street?"

"Hang on a minute," said Herb. "I didn't notice how many there were, but they did say something about moving into Grove Street later today."

"That's the new family!" said Ned.

"They were real nice and polite, too. If my wife and twin boys were stuffed into a car that small, the boys would be fighting in a minute."

"Would they make you mad?" Ned asked.

"Sure," said Herb, "but those little squabbles are just part of being a family. We all love each other anyway."

There was a crash in the driveway. Lizzie Lewis picked herself up and hurried over, wheeling a large unicycle.

"Did you find that on Grove Street?" Ned asked.

"Yes," said Lizzie. "I've been trying to find out who owns it. It's awful tough to ride. I bet my stepbrother Harry could ride it, though. Or my mom. Or my stepdad. We'd have lots of fun with it."

A little dog ran by. Pete barked and took off after it. "Pete!" said Ned, but there was no stopping him.

"I guess I'd better follow my dog," said Ned. He got back into his car.

Five blocks away, Pete was still running. He chased the other dog all the way to Ben Collins' barbershop.

Ben opened his door. "Rusty," he said, "where have you been?"

"All over the neighborhood," said Ned.

"I didn't even realize he'd sneaked out," said Ben. "He's not usually in the shop with me."

"Isn't Rusty your son John's dog?"

"John's away at school this year, and my wife Rachel's working. But my mother's come to live with us, and she usually takes care of Rusty. It's just that she went to visit a friend today."

"I bet Rusty's a great companion for your mother."

"He is," said Ben. "He's a real part of the family."

"Have you heard about the new family moving in on Grove Street?" Ned asked.

"I think the father came in for a haircut. He had a deep voice and a big black mustache."

"I knew it!" said Ned. "He's the ringmaster in the circus!"

"He didn't say," said Ben.

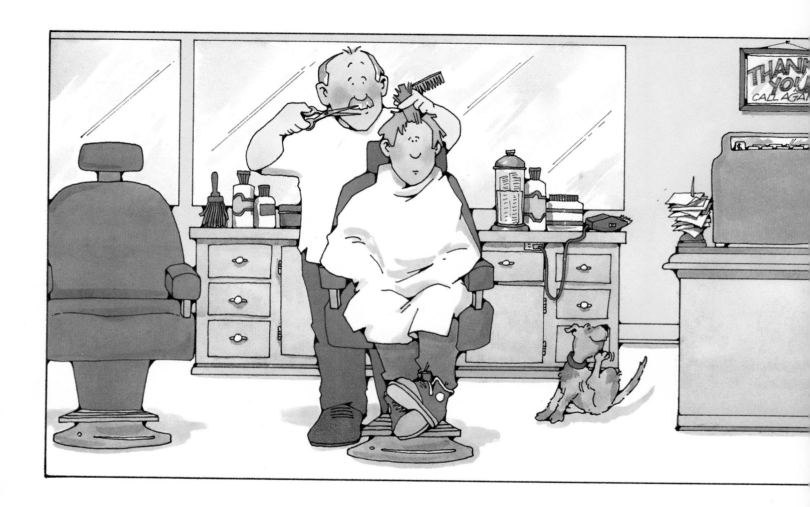

He went back to cutting Joe Miller's hair. Joe said, "You know, maybe I should get a dog for me and my dad. When one of us goes out, the other gets lonely at home by himself."

"Not a bad idea, dogs," said Ned, scratching Pete under the chin.

At that moment the little orange car went past Ben's window.

"There they go!" said Ned. "They must be moving in!"
He rushed out. Ben and Joe came with him.

By the time they reached the house on Grove Street, a
large crowd was already there. Ned saw Cathy and Ann
from the luncheonette. Officer Ollie Burns was there with

Marge and their four kids. With the twins in back, Herb and Helen Jackson had just pulled up in their pickup truck. Lizzie Lewis and her stepbrother Harry had brought the unicycle and were sitting on the curb.

The little orange car was parked beside the big van. A man got out of the car. He had a mustache, but it didn't look any different from most mustaches in Breezy Valley. A woman got out on the other side. She was pretty and looked a lot like other women in town. A regular-looking boy and girl got out, too.

"Hi," said the woman. "My name is Nancy, and I'm a music teacher. I teach a whole lot of instruments, but my son David won't practice any of them."

"I'm a gymnast," said David. "I practice on the trampoline, and I left a unicycle around here someplace."

"I'm Susan," said the little girl. She rushed over to the moving van and pulled out the largest stuffed elephant anyone had ever seen. "And this is Oscar! I collect stuffed animals."

"My name's Jim," said the man. "I'm the father."

"I don't suppose you're a ringmaster," said Newsman Ned.

"No, I'm a photographer. My studio will be right upstairs."

Newsman Ned stepped forward. "Welcome to Breezy Valley. We thought you were from the circus, but you're just different in the way all our families are different."

Jim smiled. "I hope that means we'll fit right in."

"It does," said Ned.